Food +
Farming

PAT HUTCHINS

We're Going on a Picnic!

THE BODLEY HEAD
LONDON

Also by Pat Hutchins

Rosie's Walk
The Shrinking Mouse
Don't Forget the Bacon
Ten Red Apples

A BODLEY HEAD BOOK 0 370 327551

Published in Great Britain in 2002 by The Bodley Head,
an imprint of Random House Children's Books

First published by Greenwillow Books, New York 2002

1 3 5 7 9 10 8 6 4 2

RANDOM HOUSE CHILDREN'S BOOKS
61-63 Uxbridge Rd, London W5 5SA
A division of The Random House Group Ltd.

RANDOM HOUSE AUSTRALIA (PTY) LTD
20 Alfred Street, Milsons Point, Sydney,
New South Wales 2061, Australia

RANDOM HOUSE NEW ZEALAND LTD
18 Poland Road, Glenfield, Auckland 10, New Zealand

RANDOM HOUSE (PTY) LTD
Endulini, 5A Jubilee Road, Parktown 2193, South Africa

THE RANDOM HOUSE GROUP Limited Reg. No. 954009
www.randomhouse.co.uk

A CIP catalogue record for this book is available from the British Library.

Printed in Hong Kong by Midas Printing

FOR RACHEL ISA BAINES

"Let's go on a picnic,"
said Hen, Duck, and Goose.
"It's such a lovely day!"

So Hen picked some berries
(because Hen liked berries best),
and Goose picked some apples
(because Goose liked apples best),
and Duck picked some pears
(because Duck liked pears best).
And they put them in the basket.

"We're going on a picnic!" they sang
as they walked across the field.

"This looks like a nice place
for a picnic," said Hen,
and set the basket down.
"I can't wait to eat
some of those berries!"

"It's a bit shady," said Duck.
"Let's go up the hill.
 We might find an even nicer place."
"All right," said Hen,
"but it's your turn to carry the basket."

"We're going on a picnic!" they sang
as they walked up the hill.

"This looks like a nice place for a picnic,"
said Duck, and set the basket down.
"I can't wait to eat some of those pears!"

"It's a bit windy," said Goose.
"Let's go down the hill.
  We might find an even nicer place."
"All right," said Duck,
"but it's your turn to carry the basket."

"We're going on a picnic!" they sang
as they walked down the hill.

"This looks like a nice place for a picnic,"
said Goose, and set the basket down.
"I can't wait to eat some of those apples!"

"It's a bit hot," said Hen and Duck.
"Let's go down this path.
 We might find an even nicer place."
"All right," said Goose,
"but let's ALL carry the basket."

"We're going on a picnic!" they sang
as they walked around the lane.

"Oh!" they cried,
  and set the basket down.
"We've walked back home,
  and we haven't had our picnic!"

"Off we go again," said Hen.
But when they picked up the basket,
it was very light.

And very empty.

"Duck," said Hen, "did you eat the pears?"

"No," said Duck.

"Goose," said Hen, "did you eat the apples?"

"No," said Goose.

"Hen," said Duck and Goose, "did you eat the berries?"

"No," said Hen.

"Then they must have fallen out," said everyone
    at the same time.

So Hen picked some more berries
(because Hen liked berries best),
and Goose picked some more apples
(because Goose liked apples best),
and Duck picked some more pears
(because Duck liked pears best).
And they put them in the basket.

"We're going on a picnic!" they sang
as they walked across the field.

"This looks like a nice place for a picnic,"
they all said, and set the basket down.